Hospitals Make Me Sick

Look for these SpineChillers™ Mysteries

Hospitals Make Me Sick

Fred E. Katz

Thomas Nelson, Inc.
Nashville

Published in Nashville, Tennessee, by Tommy Nelson™, a division of Thomas Nelson, Inc. SpineChillers™ Mysteries is a trademark of Thomas Nelson, Inc.

Scripture quoted from the *International Children's Bible, New Century Version,* copyright © 1983, 1986, 1988 by Word Publishing, Dallas, Texas. Used by permission.

Storyline: Tim Ayers

Library of Congress Cataloging-in-Publication Data

Katz, Fred E.
    Hospitals make me sick / Fred E. Katz.
       p. cm.—(SpineChillers mysteries ; 11)
    Summary: Michael, Scotty, and their cousin Deanna are trapped in a hospital filled with horror movie characters, but with the help of Jesus they manage to get out alive.
    ISBN 0-8499-4054-0
    [1. Hospitals—Fiction. 2. Christian life—Fiction. 3. Horror stories.] I. Title. II. Series: Katz, Fred E. SpineChillers mysteries ; 11.
PZ7.K1573Ho 1997
[Fic]—dc21

                                 97-37115
                                 CIP
                                 AC

Printed in the United States of America

97 98 99 00 01 02 QKP 9 8 7 6 5 4 3 2 1

Crash, crash, crash—ouch! were the sounds my little brother made as he dropped through the limbs of the tree. By the time I turned around, it was too late to help. Scotty lay on the thick grass holding his bleeding elbow.

Mom had brought us here from a nice, safe suburb. She couldn't wait to get us out for some of that "good country air." Although her real name is Jacqueline, everyone calls her Jackie. She's a big city real estate agent, and she's been really busy lately. She has a lot of houses for sale. Scotty and I are proud of her. She always excels at what she does. She's always taught us to do our best too.

We had borrowed this cabin in the mountains from a friend of my mom. It was only half an hour drive from our house.

When Mom's friend had dropped off the keys, she had described the cabin. She'd called it a "beautiful little log home with four bedrooms and a Jacuzzi that overlooked a river." It sounded pretty good to me, and spending the weekend with Mom sounded great.

Mom packed up the car with our suitcases, Scotty, and me. Then she told us that she had to pick up one more thing. That turned out to be our cousin, Deanna.

Deanna and I are the same age. In many ways, she's my closest friend, even though she's a girl. Deanna's the only child of Mom's twin sister. We just about grew up together since she lives just a few blocks from us. If I cut through our neighbor's backyard, it only takes me three minutes to get to Deanna's house.

My brother Scotty is two years younger than us. Scotty's the brain in the family. He is always reading some book or magazine, or even the cereal boxes in the morning. The kids at school call him "Worm" because he's such a bookworm. With his thick glasses, he even looks the part.

Scotty makes a great brother. He always has some useful bit of information for every situation we get ourselves into. But he's not perfect. In fact, he's just plain clumsy. That's how we got into our mess.

Scotty had climbed a tree because he thought he saw a rare butterfly up there. He never did find the butterfly, but he did manage to miss a limb on his climb. He made up for that by hitting all the other limbs on his way down. He fell about ten feet to the ground. He didn't break any bones, but he did have a pretty bad cut on his elbow.

Deanna and I found his glasses for him and took him back to the cabin. Mom was talking on her cellular phone. I knew it was a business call. As she talked, she pulled papers out of her briefcase and shuffled them quickly. Mom always talked a mile a minute when she was in the middle of a big deal.

This sounded like a really huge deal. She waved her arms in the air as she talked excitedly. Deanna and I helped Scotty plop down in front of Mom. It took her a few moments to notice the blood on Scotty's arm. Then the comedy started.

I thought it was hilarious to watch her race around the room holding a phone to her ear and juggling ointments and bandages. Every once in a while she made a face into the phone like the person on the other end was talking nonsense. At one point, she dropped everything and ended up trying to clean Scotty's elbow with the phone and listen to a piece of cotton.

After a few minutes Mom finally got a word in. "Listen, I'll get right back to you. An emergency has come up here." Putting her cellular phone down on the coffee table, she turned to me, as if I had hurt Scotty. "How did this happen? Why weren't you watching him?"

"Mom, he's twelve years old. He doesn't need to be watched," I answered in my defense.

3

Scotty didn't help matters as he lay on the couch moaning. Mom looked back at him and finished wiping dirt out of his cut. She asked Deanna and me, "Do you think this needs stitches?"

Behind Mom's back Scotty shook his head hard at us. I ignored him.

"Gee, Mom. That looks like an awfully deep cut. Definitely. It definitely needs stitches," I said as I suppressed a grin.

"It looks pretty bad to me," Deanna added. "All that blood's making me kind of woozy. I'm going outside while you finish bandaging him." She headed for the front door.

"I thought I saw a hospital from the highway as we drove up here. Michael James," she only used both names when she was very serious, "that was my boss on the phone. The big land deal for the mall is going through. I need to go back into the city to take care of some details. I should be gone two hours at the most."

"I'll keep everybody in line until you get back," I promised.

"No, that isn't what I meant," she explained. "We need to take Scotty to the emergency room for stitches. Would you and Deanna stay with him while I run to the city? Scotty may not get treated immediately if there are life-threatening injuries ahead of him. By the time you finish waiting in the emergency

4

room, I could probably build the mall. If by some chance you finish quickly, you can find the cafeteria and grab some lunch."

All this talk about stitches made Scotty quit moaning. By the time Mom finished talking, he was bending his arm quickly. "Look, Mom. I think it's healed already. It's a miracle!" he yelled. I thought he was going to shout "hallelujah" next.

"No, Scotty, we really should get it looked at," she told him as she smiled her don't-argue-with-me smile.

Mom threw papers into her briefcase as I put away the soap, cotton balls, washcloth, and antiseptic. Suddenly, I heard a screech from outside. Something had happened to Deanna!

Mom and I flew out the front door together. Deanna stood in the middle of the front yard pointing into the woods.

"I saw a skunk!" she yelled excitedly.

"Why the bloodcurdling scream?" Mom asked, surprised. "Skunks live in the woods. I expect we'll also see rabbits, deer, and all sorts of other wild animals up here."

Deanna looked embarrassed. "I know this is where they live, but I've never seen a skunk up close. I was afraid it would spray me," she answered in a feeble voice.

"You know, Mom, we suburbanites don't get to see many skunks," I added to take some of the heat from Deanna. "I think the only one I've ever seen is Pepe Le Pew. He's the cartoon character that keeps chasing after a poor black cat with a white stripe painted on it. You know the one; he always talks with a French accent."

Mom smiled. "Right. You kids get in the car. I'll be ready in a second," she said as she walked back toward the house to get Scotty.

"Thanks, Michael. You really covered me on that one. I feel like I'm brain dead when I do stuff like that," Deanna said as we approached Mom's sporty, yet economical American-made automobile.

"No problem. I know you'd do the same for me. What are you up for after this hospital run?" I asked.

"I could really use a quiet afternoon. I didn't sleep that well last night. It's so noisy up here. An owl kept hooting outside my window, and some kind of wild dog spent the night howling off in the woods," she answered.

"Hooting and howling? That sounds like a law firm." I went into my best TV announcer voice, "Yes, call Hooting and Howling. We'll work all night to get your case closed."

She laughed and poked me in the arm. I tried not to flinch. I don't think Deanna realizes how strong she is. She's the star on the girls' softball team. There's even a rumor at school that some professional scouts have been looking at her. Come to think of it, I bet I started that rumor. Next time, I think I'll start one about me being an alien with super powers.

I expected the drive to the hospital to be uneventful. Mom didn't know the area very well, so she asked us to watch for street signs. The roads had the most bizarre names. One was called Creepy Creek Lane. Another was named Slime Pit Road. They sounded like they belonged in my favorite kind of books: scary ones.

Scotty may be the big reader in our family, but I have a monster-sized collection of creepy novels. My favorite one is about some kids who get scared at a pizza parlor during a birthday party by all these really weird things. I wish stuff like that happened to me. Instead I lead this boring life with a super-brain brother and a super-jock cousin.

"These are some really unusual street names," Mom said, "but I know if I just keep heading south along this highway, we'll find the hospital. It can't be too far now."

Without warning, Scotty screamed into my ear, "Watch out!"

"What?" I asked, rubbing my ear.

"I saw something run across the road. It looked like a big dog, but it ran on two legs. Actually, it was kind of like a dog and a man. A dog-man," he insisted.

"That fall must have knocked a few screws loose in the old noggin, Scotty," I said.

"No, I saw it too," Deanna added with a bit of fear in her voice. "It was just like Scotty described it. Only I thought it looked more like a Wolfman. You know, like you see in monster movies."

"Maybe it was Bigfoot," I kidded.

Mom shot me that don't-kid-around look. I turned and sat up straight in my seat. Mom said to Scotty and Deanna, "I'm sure it was just a bear or something. Remember we are out in the woods."

We all quieted down as my mother turned off the highway and maneuvered her way through the dirt roads. I was starting to get drowsy, but the constant potholes we hit kept me from falling completely asleep.

I started to enter dreamland when I felt the car swerve to the right and down a hill. My eyes popped open in time to see us bounce over a gully and slip between two large trees on a dirt road. We came out of the woods and bounded back onto a paved road.

"Why did you do that?" I asked my mother.

She had a shocked look on her face as she turned her head toward me. "I saw someone in the road. He was standing right in front of me as I came around a curve. It was like he was trying to direct me to this roadway. He looked like a mountain man, with long hair and a bushy beard."

"Aunt Jackie, I can see why he directed us here. Look, it's the hospital," Deanna told us.

"It sure is, and right over there is a ramp to get back on the highway. Good. Okay, let's get you guys settled inside. I'll probably have to deal with insurance and stuff before they'll treat Scotty. And I want to make sure I can leave you here alone," she said.

10

We walked in the front door and were immediately met by a nurse. "Hello. We weren't expecting anyone this early. Have a seat and one of our staff will be right with you."

Mom smiled and asked her, "Will it take long before my son sees someone?"

"It will probably be about thirty minutes until we can begin with him," the lady in white answered.

"Hmm, I need to go into the city for a little over an hour. Can I leave the kids here if I get them set up?" Mom asked.

"Don't worry. I'll keep an eye on them. Most parents have been leaving their kids. They'll be fine," the nurse told her.

Mom looked a little confused but also relieved. "Should I pay you now or when I get back?" Mom asked.

"We're not ready to take payment yet. Go about your business and see me when you pick up the kids," the nurse answered.

"I can do that," Mom said.

"Children are why we're here," the white-dressed woman said. She turned and walked back to a counter to shuffle some papers.

Mom looked at us and said, "This seems to be working out well. I'll be back as soon as I can. All I ask is that you stay out of trouble."

"Mom, we're not little kids," I protested.

"I'm sorry. I keep forgetting that you're all in Middle School now," Mom answered with a grin.

"Mom, we don't need to stay. My elbow doesn't hurt that bad," Scotty said. He really didn't want to get stitches.

"Don't worry, Mom," I said, ignoring Scotty. "I promise to bring Scotty back in one piece. You can count on me."

Mom put her hand on my shoulder and said, "I know, Son. How about a prayer before I leave? Who would like to lead us?"

"I will, Aunt Jackie," Deanna said quickly. We bowed our heads and she prayed, "Father, we ask that you help Scotty through this, even if he has to get stitches. I hope he doesn't, but if he does, let there be as little pain as possible. I also want to pray for Aunt Jackie. Keep her safe on her ride to the city, and help her business deal go well so she can come back quickly. In Jesus' name, Amen."

"Thanks, Deanna," Mom said. "I always feel better after praying. God really is my best friend. It always helps when you can talk to your best friend."

I smiled at Mom. She turned around and walked out the door. The three of us quietly watched her leave.

Mom was barely in the car when Scotty tugged on my arm.

"I'm hungry. Can we go find something to eat while we're waiting?" he asked.

It only took me a second to respond. "Sure, I could go for a juicy burger myself. Which way?" I asked.

"That way," Scotty said. "I smell food over there."

We slipped into a hallway. I was amazed at how quiet it was here. It seemed more like a morgue than a hospital. I wished I had not had that thought.

We turned right at the end of the hall. Neither direction was lit very well. It didn't look like we were going to find someone to guide us through the maze to the cafeteria. We'd just have to guess.

The hallway got darker and darker. I thought I heard something breathing behind us. I turned around quickly, but nothing was there. I had probably just imagined it. We kept walking, and I heard it again. This time I could also feel hot breath on the back of my neck.

I spun around.

And let out a scream.

"Please, children. This is a hospital. We must be quiet, and we must stay in the appointed areas. Move along," said a very tall nurse with pasty, gray skin. She definitely could use a little sun.

I spoke quickly, "My brother cut his elbow. We're waiting for a doctor to patch him up."

As she ushered us down the hall, the spooky nurse said, "Well, you have come to the right place. We have quite a few doctors here. There is Dr. Frankenstein on the third floor and Dr. Jekyll on the second. But I don't think Dr. Jekyll is right for you. He has a terrible bedside manner. Some patients even call him beastly. It's almost as if he becomes another person. . . . Dr. Frankenstein has had plenty of experience sewing up body parts. I'll take you there."

Deanna looked at me. I looked at Scotty. Was this lady just weird, or was she trying to be funny? I almost suggested that we make a run for it when she led us through double doors into a dim hallway. I could hear other people nearby. I felt better.

15

"Now, the three of you wait right here while I go get you a doctor. Hmm, I see that you don't have your hospital bracelets or patient's gowns. I'll grab them for each of you," she told us as she left.

I tried to tell her that only my brother needed attention, but she didn't seem to hear me. I turned to the other two and said, "Is she the weirdest-looking thing you've ever seen?"

"Have you checked the mirror lately?" Scotty retorted. Then he laughed at his own joke.

"Listen, I mean it. She was strange. I don't think I like this place. Let's just get Scotty's arm patched up and wait out in the parking lot for Mom."

They agreed, and we quietly waited for the doctor. In a few minutes the nurse returned. She had hospital bracelets and gowns for us.

As she tossed them our way, she began a rapid-fire string of words. "You kids have to obey the hospital rules. Let me go over them with you.

"Number one: No bleeding on other patients.

"Number two: No cardiac arrest while on the premises.

"Number three: If any one of your limbs is severed, pack it in ice and bring it to the front desk. We'll keep it for you until you leave.

"Number four: Do not feed the Wolfman.

"Number five: Do not go outside the appointed boundaries for the patients.

"Now, go ahead and get your gowns and I.D. bracelets on. I'm going to go see what's holding up the doctor."

As she left, Deanna said, "Talk about a bad bedside manner. That woman is certainly no Mother Teresa." Deanna held up her gown. When she turned it around, I saw something on the back of the gown: a big red-and-white bull's-eye.

"Look at these gowns," I stammered. "I'm not wearing one of these."

Scotty added, "And look at these bracelets."

I looked down and read mine aloud, "John Doe. Condition: Expired."

Deanna looked at mine, then at hers. "Hey, mine is different. It says, 'Jane Doe.' But it also says that I'm expired. This hospital is treating us like spoiled milk."

I was ready to leave right then, but the doctor walked in. He had on a white coat and rubber gloves. That seemed pretty normal, but the blood splattered all over the coat and gloves didn't.

"Now, let me see what the problem is," he said.

Scotty lifted his arm. The doctor looked at it and said, "Looks like it's been bandaged well, but I better check your reaction time for any deeper damage."

He went to the big cabinet behind him and opened its doors. "I keep my reflex hammer in here somewhere. Ah, yes. Here it is," he said as he whipped

17

around holding a huge sledgehammer in the air. A bizarre smile crossed his face, and his eyes got kind of glassy.

He raised the sledgehammer in the air, and I jumped in front of my brother. "Could I see your license?" I asked.

The doctor looked right at me and said, "That would be unnecessary and unpleasant for you." Then he paused and added, "Maybe we don't need to check his reactions, but I should have a look at his throat. Let me get a tongue depressor."

The doctor dropped the sledgehammer back in the cabinet and then spun around holding a two-by-four.

"This ought to do it," he said.

Scotty shut his mouth up tight.

"All right, if you don't want good medical care then I'll send you on your way so you can solve the riddle." He wrote something out and handed it to me.

My mouth dropped open when I read it. I passed it on to Deanna, and she passed it to Scotty. It was a prescription for Fright Pills—"To be taken after every shriek."

Over the public address system we heard: "Veterinarian John Darby, please report to the front desk. The chainsaw you ordered just came in."

Scotty's doctor jumped up, "Well, that's me. Let me go get that, and we'll see if we can put it to good use on that elbow." As he left, our pasty-faced nurse returned.

"He was a veterinarian?" I asked the nurse.

"Sure, what did you expect would treat a Wolfman?" she answered.

"Now, let me take you kids back to the nonrestricted areas," she said as she prodded us out of the room and down the hall.

"Wait a second. The doctor just said that we need to solve a riddle. What did he mean?" I asked.

"My, oh my. I didn't realize that you didn't know the riddle. But then again, you didn't have your gowns and wristbands on either. Are you ready?" the nurse asked.

We nodded our heads and waited.

"What can make you laugh till you're out
    of breath
But still scare you to death?
What can help kids heal
While its fright makes you squeal?
What can raise change
While acting deranged?"

She finished her little poem and walked away.

I whispered to Deanna, "What did she mean? I really don't understand."

"I'm confused too," Deanna quietly said back to me, "but apparently Scotty doesn't need stitches. I think we should find our way out of here pronto."

"I'm with you one hundred percent. Start looking for the exit signs. We're out of here," I told her as we followed the nurse down the hallway.

The nurse was walking briskly. "Have a noose day," she called back to us. Then we heard her laughing a real horror-movie type of laugh, and she disappeared into another patient's room.

I shivered and said to the others, "Let's get out of here." We took a few steps and rounded a corner to our left. Instead of the exit, we saw a hallway filled with an eerie blue light. About ten feet from us was a group of people in hospital gowns. Their eyes seemed glazed.

The lead one saw us and grunted at us. The odd patients approached us, reaching for us. And with each step they took toward us, they moaned. We immediately turned around and started running. Unfortunately, there was another group of patients standing behind us, but their arms weren't outstretched. They couldn't be. Each patient was wearing a straitjacket.

When they saw us, they began jumping around in the hall. They yelled gibberish.

Deanna leaned close to my ear and asked, "Do you suppose they're wearing their high school letter jackets? Very nice. Don't you think?"

"This is no time for jokes," I snapped back.

Scotty had a death-grip on the back of my shirt. I turned around to see if he was okay. When I did I saw that the moaning patients had gotten closer. I looked back at the straitjacket club, and they were bouncing in our direction. They looked like giant popcorn kernels exploding in the air. Both groups were yelling. I couldn't understand what.

Suddenly, another hand grabbed me and yanked hard. I turned quickly. Deanna was pulling Scotty and me toward a utility cart as she said, "I just noticed the double doors hidden behind this cart. Looks like there's a hallway on the other side." She pushed the cart out of the way. "We've got to move quickly. Look for those red exit signs like we have at school."

We entered another long hall with several doors down each side. The hallway wasn't well lit. Then again, nothing in this hospital seemed well lit.

We ran to the end of the hall. There was another set of double doors to our left and a wide hallway to the right. We started down the hall when a group of interns stepped out of a room.

"There are some of the missing patients," one yelled. "Stop them."

"What's your prognosis, Doctor?" another asked.

"I don't know. I think we'll need to do some exploratory surgery. If we unscrew the tops of their skulls, we should be able to find the problem," the first one said with an evil laugh.

"I think we should have a consultation. Let's take them back to the examination room," a third one said.

A fourth spoke up, "And what do they wear while we consult?"

"Straitjackets!" they all answered together.

I didn't intend to wait around so these not-quite-doctors could poke around my precious brain. I grabbed the other two and pulled them back to the doors. We crashed through and fell on the floor in a heap. Our faces pressed against the hard, cold linoleum. I groaned and rolled over. When I looked up, I saw a large woman holding a long, sharp instrument hovering over us.

"We're sorry. We didn't mean to come barging in here. We were just trying to find the exit. Please, there's no need for that sharp knife," I begged.

"Hmm," she said, looking at the sharp instrument in her hand. "You're right; that's not what we have planned," she said with a bigger-than-life laugh. "How did you find your way to us? We don't get many visitors here."

As we stood up, Scotty rattled off, "First, we were chased by these glazed and dazed guys, and we ran into some weirdos in straitjackets. When we got away from them, these interns wanted to unscrew the tops of our skulls and dig around."

"I see. With so many wonderful choices, it is hard to make a decision. I'm glad you dropped by the hospital kitchen. Would you like something to eat?" she asked.

The woman motioned for us to explore the kitchen

area. I saw a group of cooks around a butcher's block cutting something up and tossing it in a big pot.

I walked a little closer to see what they were making. I hoped it looked good. Mom had told us to have lunch while we were waiting for her. I was just trying to obey her. When I got up next to the cooks, I could see what they were chopping. I wished that I hadn't.

I scurried back to Deanna's side and whispered, "You won't believe what is in that pot over there."

"Lunch, I hope," she answered. "I'm starved."

Before I could tell her, the head cook said, "Lunch is just about ready. We'll get you some food. Then you can get back to the fun. Who knows? You could be the first to find your way out. You can hang around over there." She motioned to the far wall.

We all looked at the wall and saw why she said we could hang around. There were chains and manacles dangling from the wall. Deanna said, "This is getting weird again. We have to get out of here. Even though I'm starving, I don't think I want to wait for lunch."

"You wouldn't want what was in there anyway," I said as we neared the wall.

"What were they chopping up?" she asked.

"I think it was the kids who hung around before us," I joked.

"Do you mean it was filled with . . ."

"I'm kidding, Deanna. But whatever it was, it definitely did not look edible. I say we make a run for it," I told the others. We turned to make our escape. Right behind us stood a very sweet-looking woman. She must have been more than a hundred years old. She was no more than four feet tall.

As she thrust food into our faces, she said, "I brought you some bread and jam as an appetizer."

Deanna smiled sweetly back at her. Maybe we did have the wrong idea about this place. Deanna asked, "That is great. Thank you so much, but I'm allergic to some berries. What kind of jam is this?"

The little woman held a jar close to our faces, "It's toe jam." And toes were exactly what we saw pressing against the inside of the jam jar.

Scotty gagged and turned away. I struggled to keep back a gag, but somehow Deanna kept it together and said, "On second thought, my mother always told me that it would spoil my appetite if I snacked before a meal. I think we'll just wait."

The tiny woman smiled brightly and turned away. But she mumbled to herself, "No one will try this. Maybe I should use artificial toes next time."

We stood there wondering what to do next. I had run out of ideas. I gulped and stared at the cooks. Deanna and Scotty huddled together and moved closer to me. Scotty said quietly, "I think I'm scared. I don't like this place. I want to go home."

I talked softly back to him in hopes that my voice would calm him down. "Scotty, we'll get out of here.

Remember the time we got locked in Aunt Rhonda's basement? We thought we would end up living as prisoners there the rest of our lives. Didn't we figure a way out of that one? We'll get out of this too."

The head cook slowly walked toward us with a pot of food and a big spoon. "It is always good to get another set of taste buds wrapped around your cooking. Would you kids tell me how this tastes?"

We looked at each other. Deanna spoke first, "My mother always told me not to snack before meals."

I jumped in next, "I was born without taste buds. I can't taste a thing. I wouldn't be able to help at all."

She looked at Scotty. He quickly said, "I'm his brother, and the taste bud thing is family wide."

"Well, someone has to taste this," she insisted. She moved the spoon close to my mouth and grabbed me. "If you won't eat this, you must solve the riddle."

"The riddle?" I replied.

"Yes, the riddle. To leave the hospital, answer the riddle. If you don't, you might end up on my griddle."

A man's voice boomed out beside us, "Wait! I think they would be better in the stew."

I looked in the direction of the voice and saw the largest man I had ever seen. He picked Scotty up and started to carry him away. I yelled, "Stop!"

He turned and looked at me. Scotty's face looked white. "I think he'd be a tender morsel on the menu. Don't you agree?"

"No, not at all. That little guy doesn't have much meat on his bones. On the other hand, his big brother has more than enough to go around," Deanna said.

I looked at her. I couldn't believe what she had just said. She gave me a quick look then a quick wink. She was up to something. I needed to follow Deanna's direction.

"You might have a good point there, young lady," the monster of a man said as he dropped my little brother to the floor. Scotty landed with a thump. I saw him grimace, but at least he was free. And he didn't seem to be hurt.

The big guy headed toward me, licking his lips as he approached. I looked at Deanna. If she had a plan she better put it into play right away. She slowly reached for a big can. As her hand touched it, I saw its label: vegetable oil.

Deanna grabbed the can and tipped it over. The oil oozed across the floor and slipped beneath the feet of the big guy. With his next step, his feet flew into the air and his body headed for the floor. I jumped over the oil. Scotty was on his feet and racing for the double doors. He pushed one open and stopped.

The moment I saw the straitjacket club waiting on the other side of the door, I skidded to a halt. Deanna was only a step behind me and smacked into my back.

She yelled, "Where to now?"

I did not know. Scotty let the door swing shut. The big guy was trying to get up, but he kept slipping. The head cook backed away from us, mumbling,

> "What has mirrors that wave
> And monsters that misbehave?"

As I wondered what she meant by her little rhyme, I saw another door across the kitchen. It wasn't marked, but it looked like our only way out. *Father in heaven,* I prayed, *I don't even know what's happening here. It's like we drove into another world. Please let this door be a way out.*

"This way!" I called to the others.

I took a step toward the door, but the big guy was back on his feet. "Kids, why are you afraid? Are you chicken? Maybe I could make chicken soup out of you," he said through a laugh.

Deanna looked at me and then at the oversized human being. I looked at her and then at Scotty. Scotty looked at me and then turned his head toward the straitjacket club.

Making a decision, he yelled, "Run for it!"

As Scotty ran by me, he grabbed my arm. At the same time, the big man wrapped his hairy hand around my other arm.

"He has me," I gasped. "Get out of here. I'll be right behind you." I didn't know how I would break free, but I wanted them to be safe.

I watched as Scotty and Deanna raced past the cooks who held cleavers in their hands. The kids disappeared through the door. I found myself alone in a room full of cooks. They all started heading toward me.

The big man pushed me back until I was against one of the kitchen counters. I scanned the room for some way to get free. I saw exactly what I needed.

A can of black pepper sat on the edge of the counter. *A sneeze*, I thought. *A good sneeze is just what my captor needs.* Quickly I grabbed the can and tossed pepper in his face.

The big man reared back his head and let out a monster sneeze. At the moment he sneezed, he let go of my arm. That was all I needed. I leaped for the door. It only took three steps to get there. In another second I was out of the room, but I heard the big man and the cooks talking as I left. Someone asked, "How did they get in here? I thought kids were restricted from the back of the building. I'm glad this thing is nearly over."

Scotty and Deanna were waiting for me in the hall. I didn't have a moment to think before Scotty said, "That was really weird."

"I kind of expected a kitchen like that after eating in our school cafeteria," Deanna cracked.

I laughed but didn't stay distracted for long. "Where to now?" I asked.

"We don't have much of a choice. While we were waiting for you, I looked around a little. There's a nurses' aid office down to the right but not much else. I don't know where the hallway to the left leads. I can only see as far as that corner. Maybe we should explore in that direction and look for some clues. I want to solve the riddle so we can get out of here," Deanna said.

We walked down the hallway to the left. Before we stepped around the corner, Deanna stopped us and said a quiet prayer. "Lord, we don't know what's waiting for us, but we're trusting that you're going around this corner with us."

When we continued on, we saw a figure wearing a white coat. He stood about twenty feet ahead of us.

The white coat made me think we had found a real doctor. Maybe he could help us get out of this hospital filled with horrors. I wasn't sure that he had noticed us.

"Doctor," I called.

He looked our way and then stopped. I noticed that he had one hand behind his back. He spoke to us, "I heard that we had some missing patients, and now I've found you."

"We're really not patients—I mean Scotty almost

was, but he didn't need stitches. We sure could use your help," Deanna told him.

Scotty added, "We just want to know the way out."

"You're leaving so soon? But you haven't seen the whole hospital yet." He smiled. "In fact, if you'd like to follow me . . ." Then he pulled his hand from behind his back—holding a mallet.

"No, thanks," I said. All three of us turned and bolted down the hall. I realized we could go back to the kitchen and end up as Today's Luncheon Special, or we could head for the nurses' aid office. I chose the second and quickly motioned for the others to follow me.

I could hear the doctor calling to us as we raced around the corner, "No, wait. That's the wrong way. All the real fun is in the front of the building. I'll show you where. Come back."

We reached the office, pushed the door open, leaped inside, and noiselessly closed the door behind us. I could hear the doctor's footsteps as he ran by. He must not have seen us enter this office. We sat with our backs against the door. I sighed.

"That was another close one," I said quietly. I didn't want that doctor to hear me and come after us. "Are you starting to get the sense that there is something very unusual about this place? And what did that doctor mean by all the real fun being in the front of the building?"

Then I realized Deanna was tugging on my arm.

"What is it, Deanna?" I asked.

"We're not alone," she whispered.

"I know we're not alone. There are probably hundreds of people in this hospital. Of course, we are not alone," I snapped at her. I could tell that I was a little stressed out. I was not usually this grumpy.

"No, I mean in this room," she said back to me. Deanna pointed. Across the room from us, a nurse stood in front of a counter sorting through pill bottles. Her back was turned to us.

Scotty let out a small whimper of fear. I leaned near him and said, "It's a nurse. Everything's okay. We can ask her how to get out of this horrible hospital."

We stood up and walked quietly to the other side of the room. I cleared my throat to get the nurse's attention. She did not turn around.

I cleared my throat again. Again I got no reaction. Deanna pushed her way around me. "About the only thing you'll get that way is a cough drop," she hissed at me. Deanna reached out, tapped the nurse's arm, and said, "Excuse me, but could you tell us how to get out of this place?"

"Have you solved the riddle?" the nurse questioned without turning around.

"Why do we have to solve a stupid riddle just to get out of here?" I asked.

"Because you're in a hospital and you have to obey hospital rules. I suppose I could give you a hint. Let's see:

36

'Dressed in green
They improve the scene.
Dressed today
They pretend they're mean.'"

I sighed and said, "That really doesn't help at all. Couldn't you just pretend you're the information desk and point the way out?"

Instead of responding, the nurse slowly turned toward us. It only took me a second to recognize the Bride of Frankenstein.

"Ahhhh!" Scotty screamed. I was pretty sure that the hair on the back of my neck raised up.

"Run!" I yelled. We bolted toward the door.

The hallway was clear. I stopped the others, looked both ways to make sure nothing was chasing us, and said, "That's enough of this. We need to solve that riddle so we can get out of here. Does anybody remember it all?"

Of course, Scotty the Brain remembered it perfectly. Like I said, sometimes he makes a pretty useful little brother. Scotty recited:

> "What can make you laugh till you're out
>   of breath
> But still scare you to death?
> What can help kids heal
> While its fright makes you squeal?
> What can raise change
> While acting deranged?"

"I can say it, but I have no idea what it means, he said."

"Add what the nurse told us and we still have nothing," I said in surrender.

"Let's think about it for a second. We're not being chased. There aren't any creeps in straitjackets around us, and Frankenstein's Bride chose not to follow us. Scotty, what's that first part again?" Deanna asked.

"What can make you laugh till you're out of breath but still scare you to death?"

"Not much in this place makes me laugh," I snorted.

"So far everything scares me to death," Scotty added.

"Think about it. What makes you laugh?" Deanna asked again.

"Comedians."

"TV shows."

"Michael's face," Scotty said, and I shot him my big-brother-is-going-to-put-frogs-in-your-lunch look.

I added, "Comic books."

"Comic strips in the newspaper," Deanna threw in. Then she said, "This is getting us nowhere. None of those can make us laugh and scare us to death at the same time. And none of them are here. What's the next part?"

"What can help kids heal while its fright makes

you squeal? What can raise change while acting deranged?" Scotty repeated.

"Beats me. Maybe what the big guy in the kitchen said will help," I added. "How did it go? What has mirrors that wave and monsters that misbehave?"

"Some carnivals have wavy mirrors," Scotty answered.

"But what does that have to do with a hospital?" Deanna asked.

"I'm stumped," I told them. "Maybe we should try to search for more clues. Which way do we go?"

"I'm beginning to think that we should go back out to the front," Deanna said.

"That sounds as good as anything else," I answered. "Let's go." We headed down the winding corridor and turned at least two corners before we came to a door with any kind of marking on it.

Deanna read the sign out loud, "Organ Donors Needed. Enter Here."

"Do people just walk in there and say, 'I want to donate my liver. Can you take it out, please?'" I kidded.

"Don't be goofy. That's probably just where people pick up the paperwork for donating their organs. They don't take them out until after you die," Scotty retorted.

Deanna grabbed the door handle and said, "Then there's probably not much in here."

Before I could stop her, she pushed the door open and walked in. She checked out the room, looked back at us over her shoulder, and said, "Hey, you two have got to see this."

I pushed past Scotty into the room. I looked around, surprised. The room was filled with organs. The kind of organs that have keyboards and foot pedals. I immediately laughed. Maybe this hospital was not as scary as we all thought. Maybe this was a clue.

"I can't believe this," Scotty said behind me. "This has to be a joke."

"I was just thinking the same thing. If we can find someone in here, maybe we can get some help," I suggested.

"I can't see much of anything besides organs," Deanna said.

"I think I see two pathways between the instruments," Scotty said.

"I see them too," I answered.

"Let's go explore," Deanna added. "You two go that way. I'll follow this one. The first one to find anybody screams." She giggled nervously.

Scotty and I wove our way through the stacked organs. After several minutes of weaving in and out, I felt completely turned around. Scotty started to ask me a question, but I shushed him.

Then I whispered, "Quiet. I heard something over

there." We stopped dead in our tracks and listened. The other sound stopped as well.

I motioned to Scotty, and we took a few steps. I heard something ahead of us take a few steps too. Up ahead the path between the organs made a right turn. It didn't take a brain surgeon to figure out that we might be about to meet the keeper of the organs.

"Scotty, I'm going to jump around that corner," I whispered. "If something grabs me, scream for Deanna and then run." I took a breath and leaped around the corner of stacked organs.

I stood with my hands up and ready to fight. I stared, startled, then I broke into deep laughter. The keeper of the organs was only Deanna.

"Did you see anything scary?" she asked.

"Only you," I answered.

"Where's Scotty?"

"Waiting back there." I pointed behind me. "Hey, Scotty, it's only Deanna. Come on around," I called. Nothing happened. Scotty didn't come. I called again louder, "Scotty!" He didn't answer.

"This is giving me major creeps," Deanna said. "Let's go get him."

We walked toward where I'd left my brother. Scotty was gone!

"Scotty!" Deanna yelled. "Where are you?"

All we heard was silence. We ran between the organs. One of the instruments had been moved, and we saw a new pathway.

"This wasn't here before. Something must have grabbed Scotty. I'll bet he went through here. We've got to find him," I insisted.

We followed the new path, and it only took us a second to find Scotty and a doctor. At least, I thought it was a doctor. He was dressed in a white jacket, but the rest of him defied the description of any doctor I had ever seen.

The doctor's back was raised in a hump. His skin was gray, one eye poked out of his face, and the other one was almost closed.

The doctor pulled Scotty closer to him. He slurred and slobbered, "I'm so glad you came in. I don't get many customers. Are you here to donate an organ?"

"Uh, no," I answered.

"Then perhaps you're here to receive an organ," the doctor said. Without warning he tossed a heart toward Deanna. It bounced on the floor as Deanna screamed.

The doctor laughed an evil laugh as he explained the heart was made of rubber.

Scotty quietly moaned, "I want to leave this place."

"You've got to solve the riddle first," the doctor replied. "Perhaps you need a hint:

'What raises funds
While giving fun
And causes fear
When it appears?'"

When he finished the riddle, the doctor pushed Scotty toward me and reached behind an organ. The next thing I saw was a chainsaw outlined against the doctor's white coat.

"Since you allowed one of my favorite donations to fall to the floor, I'll need to withdraw something equal to it—times three," the weird doctor said.

Scotty whimpered.

Deanna gasped then yelled, "Let's split before he splits us."

She took off through the maze of musical instruments. My brother and I were only a half step behind her. We could hear the demented doctor calling after us. We couldn't find the door, but Scotty spotted a place to hide and catch our breath.

"I don't think we were playing his tune," Deanna whispered with a giggle. "I think he wanted to offer us aggressive medical treatment."

I kind of smiled, but I wasn't in the mood for lame jokes. Deanna kept on whispering. "Do you think I broke his heart?"

"What?" I answered as I furrowed my eyebrows in confusion.

"I mean when I let the heart fall on the floor," she giggled again.

"Deanna, why are you always making jokes?" I asked in frustration. "We should be concentrating on getting out of here."

"Haven't you ever heard of the healing power of humor?" she replied, still giggling.

Before I could answer, we heard the organ center's door open and close. It sounded very close, but so was whatever had come through it.

Scotty whispered to us, "I felt a breeze when the door shut. I'll bet it's right on the other side of this wall of organs."

"All we have to do is climb over. Once we get to the door, we'll be safe," I said.

Deanna added, "But who knows what's lurking in the hallway?"

I sighed. She had a good point. But we had to

choose between the hallway and all the weirdos out there or Dr. Chainsaw. I chose the hallway. "Let's pray for our safety," I suggested.

Scotty and Deanna bowed their heads with me, and I whispered, "Lord, this place is totally bizarre. It's like we're in some kind of fun house. But Father, we're not having any fun. We could use your help in getting out of this room safely. Please protect us from whatever may be in the hallway. Thank you. Amen."

I opened my eyes and said, "I'll climb to the top of the organs first and help you two up. Jump down and get out of here fast. Okay? Let's go!"

I scrambled out of our hiding place and up the wall of organs. Each one screamed out a horrible note as I stepped on its keyboard. Dr. Chainsaw would know exactly where we were. I had to do this quickly.

From the top I couldn't see anyone on the other side of the stack. That was a good sign. But when I looked back toward Scotty and Deanna, I saw the hunchbacked doctor racing toward us through the maze.

I reached down, grabbed Scotty by the collar, and pulled him up. As I dropped him on the other side of the stack, I said, "Get the door open. I'll help Deanna." Deanna rarely needed help with anything, but when she saw the doctor coming, she willingly held up her hands for help. I reached out and grabbed her as the hunchback with the chainsaw scrambled onto the bottom organ's keyboard.

He yelled up at us, "Please, kids, you could help us save lives by donating an organ."

Then he cryptically added,

"Donate your organ,
And we'll all have fun.
Then I can fix those
Of another one."

I shook my head. He seemed to be giving us another clue, but his rhyme made as little sense as all the other ones had.

"Deanna, we have to get out of here," I said urgently as I gave a powerful yank. She almost flew over the organs, but I caught her. Deanna's feet crashed on a keyboard as she climbed down. She was safe, but Dr. Chainsaw was only inches from climbing up to me. In my heart, I screamed to God for help.

Deanna dropped to the floor and raced into the hallway. I had to be quick too. I couldn't just jump— I was up too high and I'd probably break an ankle or something. Then I saw my way down. An exit sign stuck out of the wall above the door. If I jumped down and grabbed it to slow my fall, I could land safely.

There wasn't a second to lose. I leaped.

My hands smashed into the sign as I tried to slow my fall. I held on, but the sign didn't. It creaked and bent, and I dipped six inches closer to the floor. I let go and landed with my sneakers firmly planted in the running position. I tore through the door, and Scotty let it slam shut.

Deanna motioned for us to follow her. She probably had no idea where we were going, but all I cared about was getting farther away from the organs.

Deanna skidded to a stop ahead of us. She pushed a door open and disappeared through it. I didn't even stop to read the sign. I ran through behind her with Scotty at my heels.

We all leaned against the wall gasping for breath. Deanna spoke first, "Help me remember that I don't ever want to take organ lessons."

I gave a short snort of a laugh. Then I asked, "Where are we?"

Scotty looked up and saw shelves and shelves of books. "It's a library!" he said.

Our resident bookworm had already moved to the first shelf. He turned around and said, "You have got to see these titles. They're all kids' books. And every one sounds spooky."

Deanna and I each walked to different shelves.

"Listen to this title," I said. *"Midnight on Creepy Creek."*

"I've read that. It's a great book," Deanna said.

We all started reading titles to one another.

"My Hollywood Scream Test."

"Draw Your Blood. It looks like it's about art class."

"Santa Claws Is Coming, but *Claus* is spelled C-L-A-W-S."

"Old MacDonald's Fear Farm."

"The Exterminator Bugs Me."

"A Shocker at Soccer."

"Dead Again . . . And Again . . . And Again."

"Tales of Middle School Terror. This one I don't want to read. It sounds too close to the truth."

"Nighty Night, Sleep Fright."

"Attack of the 60-Foot Principal."

"It Came from Beneath My Bed. It must be about your bed, Scotty."

"The Haunted Pizza."

"Our Guest Room Is Haunted."

Deanna responded to that title with a laugh and said, "Now, you guys tell me."

52

"The Uninvited Guest."

"The Sleepover from Beyond."

"Moving Can Be Murder."

"Here's another one that I don't think I want to read. It's called *Hospitals Make Me Sick,*" I said with a shiver.

As he and Deanna came closer to see the book, Scotty asked, "What's it about? This could be our guide out of here."

Scotty took the book from me and flipped it open. He skimmed a few pages then said, "It's about three kids who get stuck inside a hospital filled with monsters and maniac doctors."

"Sounds too true to life for me," Deanna responded.

Then we heard the door open. Someone entered humming a tune. I recognized the song from the old TV show *The Munsters*. "Duck down," I whispered.

We hit the floor.

Deanna whispered, "Keep reading. Maybe it will tell us how to get out of here."

"I hear talking. Who is talking in my library?" asked a high-pitched, nasal voice. "This is a quiet zone." The voice sounded like it was right above us. We looked up at the librarian and scrambled to our feet. Scotty accidentally kicked the book, and it flew under a shelf.

The librarian wore her hair pulled back in a bun. Big thick glasses perched at the end of her nose, and they were attached to a gaudy gold chain that went around her neck.

"You have forgotten the cardinal rule of libraries: If you talk, you must be punished. Follow me," she said in a very harsh manner.

Deanna asked, "What will our punishment be?"

"The same one that I give to all my talkers." The librarian stopped. "Now, where is the perfect book for all of you? It seems to be missing. It should be right here." She motioned to the empty spot where I had found *Hospitals Make Me Sick.*

11

Scotty and Deanna looked at me. The one place that we had thought would be safe, wasn't. As the librarian scurried around looking for the book, we turned and ran as fast as we could. We yanked the door open and dashed back into the hallway.

When he was sure the librarian wasn't following us, Scotty stopped. "Wait a second. We need to talk," he said in an unusually serious voice.

"What is it, Scotty?" I was worried.

"That book the librarian was looking for . . . it was *Hospitals Make Me Sick,* wasn't it? I didn't get a chance to read much of it, but I did see some very scary things," he said slowly.

"Like what?" Deanna asked as her hand went to his shoulder.

"Like I told you in there, it was about three kids lost in a hospital of horror," Scotty told us as he shook his head in disbelief.

"That's just a coincidence. Lots of books have three characters," I assured him.

"But the hospital . . . everything about the book made me think it was about us," he said seriously.

Deanna slid closer, "Scotty, did you happen to see how the story ended?"

"I didn't get that far because the librarian came in," he answered. "All I got was that they were in the emergency room. Maybe we should find the emergency room," he suggested.

"What happens in the emergency room? Do the characters become eternal patients at the hospital, or do they escape?" Deanna asked with rising agitation.

"I don't know. They were about to solve some kind of riddle," he said.

"One of our riddles? What was the answer?" I pressed.

He shook his head to say that he didn't know.

"I'm going back for the book," Deanna said. "We've got to get the answer to the riddle."

"No, that's too dangerous. The librarian's still in there," I said. Then I heard something. "Listen, I hear steps coming down the hall. We have to find a place to hide," I added as I twisted my head from side to side searching for safety. The steps got closer. We did not have much time to waste.

"Follow me," Deanna said. We ran down the hallway away from the approaching footsteps.

Deanna pointed to a sign up ahead and read it out loud: "Deliveries." Over her shoulder, she said,

"That must be where medical supplies are delivered. Maybe it will lead us to a loading dock and a way outside."

We crashed through the door expecting to see blue sky and trees. Instead we came face to face with two doctors and a nurse. We just stared at them. One of the doctors picked up a surgical tool and walked toward us. As he got closer, I could see that he held a scalpel. We were in trouble again.

I spoke up, "Sorry, we seem to have walked into the wrong room. We'll be on our way."

Scotty, Deanna, and I backed toward the door. One of the doctors stepped forward and said, "Please, don't hurry out. We're just waiting for a routine delivery here. You don't have to leave."

The nurse chirped in, "You three look scared. Is everything okay?"

Scotty and Deanna looked at me. We couldn't believe we had finally found some normal medical staff. I felt my body relax. Maybe all this weirdness had come to an end.

"This has been a really bizarre day," Deanna told them. "We've been chased by orderlies and patients in straitjackets and crazy doctors, and everyone wants us to solve some riddles, but we can't figure them out."

"Don't forget the guy with the organs," Scotty added.

First one doctor laughed, then the other one did. Finally the nurse's giggle became loud laughter too. We were confused. One of the doctors gained his composure for a moment and said, "Right. The riddles. We've got one of our own:

'What makes kids well quick
While making you kids "sick"?'"

"Hospitals," I answered. "Hospitals make me sick."

"Very good. There's just . . ." Suddenly the doors behind us crashed open, and a guy carrying a pizza walked in.

"Delivery!" he yelled. "One large deluxe pizza."

"That's why the sign outside says Deliveries. This is where we get our pizzas delivered," the nurse explained.

I could hardly believe it, but this was getting nuttier. As I stood staring at the pizza, I saw the top of the box bow upward.

The top flew off. In the center of the pizza stood a creature. Its mouth opened and closed beneath a long lizardlike nose. Two round, yellow eyes stared at us.

Scotty squeaked.

Deanna pulled my arm. Then she pointed at a door just beyond the doctors. "Let's go, Michael. I don't want to wait and see if that pizza has pepperoni that dances too."

We quickly edged across the floor away from the pizza with extra creeps. As we passed the doctors, one grabbed for Deanna. She spun to her left and eluded the grasp.

Scotty wasn't as fortunate. The bigger of the two doctors wrapped his hairy hand inside Scotty's collar. I had to think of something quick.

The slippery polished floor was perfect for my plan. I was the best base runner on our softball team because my Uncle Tony had taught me how to slide. I put that knowledge into practice and flew head first along the floor.

I had gotten my speed up while running and the slide was powerful. When I flew by my brother, I grabbed his ankle. He went down on his belly, but my momentum pulled him along with me.

We stopped a foot from the door. Deanna grabbed us both and yanked us up. Then we sped through the exit and tumbled onto soft, comfortable carpet.

Behind us I could hear the crazy nurse calling, "Wait a second. We can help you solve the riddle."

I rolled three times across the plush floor and bumped into a wall. Scotty and Deanna thumped down behind me.

Deanna scrambled to her feet and grabbed Scotty's arm. They both helped me up and leaned my back against the wall. The wall felt cool, like glass. I turned my head to check it out.

"It's the nursery for newborn babies!" I exclaimed. The other two already knew. They were staring through the window. There were several rows of baby cribs. I looked inside expecting to see cute little faces. I guess I had forgotten where I was. This wasn't a cute-little-face kind of hospital.

The cribs did not have babies in them. Each crib had a very large egg in it. "I don't think I've ever seen eggs that big before," I told the others.

"I saw one in a movie once. It turned out to be a dinosaur egg," Deanna said.

"Dinosaur eggs do not exist except as fossils. In fact, I don't think there are any animals alive today that lay eggs that size. My guess is that these are from a very rare, genetically altered beast," Scotty said.

"Fine," I told him. "Tell me, Dr. Science, what do you propose we do about these eggs? Do we leave them alone so they can hatch and maybe eat the town? Or do we destroy them?"

"I'm never for the destruction of life. I think we should just tiptoe on out of here," Deanna said.

"Too late," Scotty said.

Deanna and I took another look at the eggs. Several had started to rock back and forth. Then one began to crack across the top.

"I really don't want to see what comes out of those things," Deanna said. "Let's get out of here."

I didn't even stop to agree. I just ran after my cousin.

As usual, Deanna was way ahead of Scotty and me. She chose a door and went flying through it. I figured we had little choice in the matter but to follow her. The key to making it out of the hospital was to stay together.

Above the door, the sign read Nurses' Station.

Scotty and I approached the door more slowly than Deanna had. I had become cautious because of all the strange things we'd encountered. I pushed the door open and found Deanna talking to a nurse. I got a little scared because the nurse had her back to Deanna. We had seen this before, and the last time it hadn't been good.

I heard the nurse say, "Go through this door, take the hallway until it ends, and then turn left. You will see a big red door. On the other side of that door is what you are looking for."

"Thanks," I told her.

I think my voice startled her because she quickly turned. I jumped. The nurse was our old friend, the Bride of Frankenstein.

Scotty reached for the door handle, but that escape route was cut off by two large orderlies who had silently joined us. Scotty looked like someone had just punched him in the stomach.

"What is this?" I asked. "Why has the whole staff of this hospital gone crazy?"

The nurse answered, "We all have a 'staph' infection." Then she giggled.

Bewildered by the stupid joke, I looked at Scotty. He put his hand on my shoulder. I felt it shaking. He was very scared. Then I remembered that God promised to be with me always. He knew what was going on. I prayed for direction. *Lord, I have no idea how to get out of this. We really need your help.* The orderlies pushed their way into the room, and the nurse approached us slowly as I prayed.

I saw that Deanna was standing next to a bowl of sponges. That gave me an idea. "Deanna, I just can't *absorb* all this. I'm feeling *soft and spongy* inside." I hoped that she would catch my hints.

Deanna looked at me strangely. At first she did not understand. But then she saw the sponges, and I saw her smile.

She leaped toward the bowl and grabbed it, flinging sponges all over the floor. I grabbed a few and started tossing them at the medical staff.

The nurse caught a sponge and turned her eyes my way. "Why are you doing this? We just want to give you some TLC."

Scotty asked me, "What is TLC?"

The nurse answered him, "The *T* stands for terror, and the *L* stands for . . ."

I interrupted her, "I think I've heard enough already. Let's get out of here!"

Deanna and I grabbed Scotty and dragged him with us as we left. We raced down another hallway. I looked for a place to hide and figure out an escape plan.

Up ahead was a door marked Laundry. If we made it there, we might be safe for a while. We were only a few yards from the door.

14

We all heard the clatter in the hallway at the same time. We barely got through the door marked Level 2 Laundry before the hall filled with people. I held my breath and listened.

"I'm sure I heard them run down this way. We've got to find those three. They're the only 'patients' in this part of the hospital," said a voice in the hallway.

"Someone check the laundry room," said another.

"Quick, jump in this laundry basket and cover yourselves with sheets," Deanna whispered.

Neither Scotty nor I argued. When the door opened, we were hidden securely. The woman who opened the door called back to the others, "Nothing in here." She shut off the light, closed the door, and we were left alone in the dark.

"I guess we're safe for now," I whispered. "And we've got some time to think things through. Does anyone have any idea what's going on?"

"I've been thinking," Scotty answered. "Maybe everything we've seen can be explained."

"What do you mean?" I asked.

"Well, that creature on the pizza looked a lot like a puppet. It could've been the delivery dude's hand," he said. "And we didn't stick around to see what came out of those eggs. Maybe they were fake too."

"That makes sense. Maybe the doctors are faking the scary stuff too. They might all just be wearing monster movie-style make-up," Deanna added.

"That could be part of the answer to the riddle. You know:

> 'What can raise change
> While acting deranged?'

"The doctors and nurses are acting deranged," Scotty said. He sounded close to solving the riddle.

"But how are deranged doctors going to raise change? And what are they planning to change?" I asked, confused.

"I'm not sure yet," Scotty told me.

"What did Dr. Chainsaw in the room full of organs tell us?" Deanna asked.

Scotty answered,

> "Donate your organ,
> And we'll all have fun.
> Then I can fix those
> Of another one."

He stopped for a moment and then said, "Hey, maybe they're going to use those donated organs for something fun."

"What about the last clue we got?" I asked. "Scotty, do you remember how it went?"

"I think it was

'What makes kids well quick
While making you kids "sick"?'

"But I don't see how our getting sick can help kids get well quick," he answered.

"I don't get it. My head's starting to hurt. Let's see if we can figure out how to get out of here, with or without the solutions to the riddles," I said.

"How about if we start by finding the light switch," Deanna said. She rustled around in the room until she found the switch by the door.

We didn't see much besides dirty sheets, pillow-cases, and stuff. I looked around and found surgical scrubs. But the outfit was really huge. I wondered if King Kong had worn it.

Then I got an idea. "I have a plan," I said pantomiming a cartoon lightbulb over my head. "I found a set of doctor's scrubs. They're really big. I bet two of us could pretend to be one orderly. Scotty, sit on my shoulders and you can be the head. I'll be the legs, but you'll have to direct me."

"What about me?" Deanna pleaded.

"I have that figured out too."

"So what's my role in the Great Horror Hospital Escape?" she asked.

"You, my dear cousin, will be going for a ride. You can hide inside the cart, and we'll push it down the hall. We'll just keep pushing it until we find an exit. In our disguise, no one will hassle us," I told them both.

I pulled on the surgical pants, and then Scotty scrambled up on my shoulders. He was already wearing the shirt.

Deanna jumped into the cart and started complaining. "Whoa, it's cramped in here."

Her complaints made Scotty doubt my plan. "Michael, what makes you think this crazy idea will work?"

"I saw it in a movie once. A group of guys tried to escape from jail this way," I answered.

"Did it work?" Deanna said.

"I don't know. I fell asleep before the end," I told them as I approached the door. "Maybe we should say a quick prayer for our safety," I added. The others nodded, and we bowed our heads in silence for a moment. Then I smiled and said, "Remember, Scotty, we have to act like we're one doctor—and Deanna, no noise."

"Wait a second," Scotty said as I was about to open the door. "I found something in this shirt's pocket."

"What?" I mumbled. My position below him had already started to get hot.

"It's a ticket," he answered.

Deanna reached up and took it from his hand. "The kid's half right, Michael. It's half a ticket. And there's writing on it."

"What can you read?" I asked.

"It says 'horror f' on the top line and 'for kids' on the bottom line," she told us.

"Horror for kids is exactly what this place is all about," I scoffed.

"What about that *f* after horror? What word could it have started?" Scotty asked.

"Let's figure it out after we've escaped this loony hospital," I told them as we started into the hall.

The hall was relatively quiet. I could see through a small rip in the surgical shirt that hung down over my face. I walked toward the end of the hall while Scotty pushed the cart. Scotty was whispering down the shirt at me.

"Michael, there's someone in the hall. What do I do now?"

I couldn't answer him before a voice boomed at us. "Excuse me, but I'm looking for three patients. Have you seen three kids run this way?"

Scotty attempted to lower his voice to answer the question. "Nope, haven't seen a thing." Unfortunately, my brainy brother has trouble walking and chewing gum.

He lost his balance and tumbled forward into the cart. Scotty's momentum sent us flying down the hall. I had to run to keep up with the cart. My running only made the cart roll faster and faster. I had no choice but to leap inside and go along for the ride.

Several people began chasing us. I didn't think they could catch up. Then I saw that we were quickly coming to the end of the hallway. We had to turn right or left or we'd hit the wall.

"Everybody! Lean to your left," I yelled.

We leaned, and the cart tipped up so only its two left wheels were still on the floor. My idea worked; we made a hard turn. We flew down the hall. We were coming to a dead end, but I spied a laundry chute in the wall.

"Change of plans. This cart is going to ram that wall in about thirty seconds. Be prepared to jump through that laundry chute. Deanna, leap before we hit. Scotty, leap when we hit, and I'll follow you."

A second later, Deanna jumped through the chute door. The moment we smashed against the wall, my brother flew through the air. I was glad that he had taken diving lessons. In spite of his clutziness, his form looked pretty good.

I braced myself for the whiplash from the impact. The momentum of the cart hurtled me into the air and down the chute. The chute was dark. It seemed a lot longer than I had planned on. The next thing I heard was Scotty.

"Argh!" he yelled as he hit bottom. Deanna had dropped before him. Like a rocket, I shot over them, thudding into the dirty laundry below. We had all landed safely.

I lay on my back in the soft laundry and sucked in a deep breath. "Isn't it great when a plan works?" I asked with a grin.

I think I pushed them a little too far. Deanna grabbed a towel and snapped me with it. "Why do I go along with your wild and crazy plans? The next time, you need to watch the end of the movie and see if the plan actually works."

Scotty got up. "We're safe, and that's all that counts."

"Thanks, Scotty. You're right. Now we need to find out where we are," I added as my eyes darted around the small room.

"Well, since we fell an awfully long way, I bet we're in the basement," my genius brother said.

"Okay, so how do we get out?" Deanna asked.

I suggested we explore the basement.

We climbed out of the dirty laundry and walked past the washing machines and dryers. We found a closed door. Deanna hesitated before she opened it. All three of us were getting tense about what might be lurking behind closed doors. Finally, she yanked it open.

Deanna turned around and winked at me. Nothing but an empty corridor.

16

"Look, I see a flashing neon sign for a blood bank," Deanna said with a grin, as we walked the corridor.

"A neon sign!" exclaimed my brother. "Don't you think a neon sign on a blood bank is a little tacky?"

But Deanna, already halfway down the hall, ignored his remark. She saw something on the wall that made her turn back toward us. "Hey, you have got to see this poster," she said.

Scotty and I quickly joined her. We both started laughing at the poster for the blood bank. It had a picture of Dracula saying, "Come in and let me make a withdrawal."

"This place has a sense of humor," Scotty said. Then he recited,

> "What can make you laugh till you're out
> of breath
> But still scare you to death?

"Maybe this is part of the solution," he said,

concentration showing on his face. "The riddle has to be about the hospital."

"You might be right," I answered. "But I really just want to get out of here. I don't care about the silly riddles anymore.

"I hope the basement is off limits to the weirdos from upstairs. Maybe there's someone inside who can show us the exit."

We pushed the door open and cautiously entered. I took one look at the man behind the desk and stopped. My mouth dropped open, and I whispered, "The poster wasn't a joke. That guy *is* Dracula!"

I pointed at the man sitting behind the desk. He wore a long black cape and had glossy, black hair that came to a peak in the center of his forehead. He smiled at us. I wished he hadn't. Long fangs poked out of his mouth.

He lifted his head and spoke in a strange accent. He actually sounded more like the Count from *Sesame Street* than any movie Dracula I'd ever seen.

"Well, good afternoon, children," he said. "How can I help you? Are you here to make a deposit? It will hardly even hurt. I'll just make a small puncture to remove your blood." Then he broke into a spooky laugh.

"Well, not exactly," I told him after I gulped in a breath. "We were just peeking in." I could feel my hands breaking into a cold sweat.

"Please come in and let me show you around," he offered.

"That's all right. I think we'll just move on. Could you tell us how to get out of the hospital?" I asked.

We were backing toward the door when I heard Deanna let out a quiet gasp. I was afraid to turn around. But I had to.

Behind us stood the doctor who had looked at Scotty's elbow when we first came in. "There you are. We've been looking all over the hospital for you three. I'm the doctor in charge of the blood bank," he said with a sinister gleam in his eyes.

"We were just leaving," Deanna said as she tried to push by him.

"Why? You could be such a big help . . ."

Deanna put up her hand and motioned for the doctor to keep away from her. She told him, "I don't think we should give blood. We all have a . . . a rare disease."

Scotty started to say that he didn't have any kind of disease, but Deanna furtively stomped on his toes. He got the message and shut up.

"All three of you have the same disease?" the doctor asked in disbelief.

I jumped in, "It's because we're cousins."

While we talked to the doctor, we did not notice that the horror movie escapee had slipped up behind us. Dracula grabbed me from behind. The doctor reached out and snagged Deanna. Caught!

Scotty surprised me. He slithered away from us and our two captors. I had no idea what he was about to do. He leaped on top of the desk and announced in a very commanding voice, "Let go of them, or you will experience the wrath of Ultraboy." It totally shocked me. It seemed so unlike Scotty.

Everyone stared. I was the only one who knew that Ultraboy was a cartoon character Scotty liked to draw. He made all these little comic books with Ultraboy as the hero. I almost laughed. Then I noticed that the doctor and Dracula had stunned looks on their faces. They released their grips on us, and Deanna and I pulled away from them.

Dracula turned to Scotty and warned, "Now, please settle down. I'm not here to hurt you. We're here to amuse you. Help me, doctor." They both stepped in Scotty's direction. He had saved us—what could Deanna and I do to help him?

The two men grabbed for Scotty. He surprised

me one more time by leaping into the air above Dracula's head. He grabbed onto a ceiling fan. I was glad it wasn't moving or we would have had to take him home in slices. I would've had a mega-tough time explaining that to Mom. Scotty used the fan to swing over their heads. The next thing I knew, he dropped from the fan and landed right beside me.

"All right, Ultraboy!" Deanna exclaimed.

We grabbed him and raced into the hallway again. I slapped Scotty on the back and said, "Way to go, Scotty. I was waiting for Ultraboy to use his super-powers, though."

"I don't know what came over me," he told us as he shook his head. "I realized that I needed to do something quick. I asked myself what Ultraboy would do in a situation like this. And then I did it."

"I'm glad that you did. Let's get out of here," I said as I herded the others down the hallway. Something caught Scotty's eye. He skidded and stared at a sign. It said: "Come In. We Want to Keep an Eye on Your Health."

"I want to see what's in here," Scotty told us.

"Are you nuts?" I asked a little too loudly. There was a degree of frustration in my voice.

"Don't worry. You have Ultraboy with you," he responded and stuck out his chest.

"Ultra, smultra. We are not going in there!" I exclaimed.

I hardly had the last syllable out of my mouth when Ultraboy opened the door. I looked inside. It was dark. Scotty and Deanna went in anyway. I stood in the hallway. I was not about to follow them . . . until I heard loud talking coming toward me in the hallway. I had no choice. I had to get out of sight, and I had to do it quickly. I pushed the door open. I half-expected to see my brother and cousin in the grasp of some creature.

Instead, I found myself alone in a fairly dark room. Scotty and Deanna were gone. When the door swung shut behind me, the tiny bit of gray light from the hallway disappeared. I stood alone in the pitch blackness.

"Scotty," I said in a stage whisper. I didn't want the people in the hall to hear me. No answer came back.

"Listen, Ultraboy," I whispered. "If there was ever a time to come to the rescue of your brother, this is it." No answer again.

A tiny light came on. In front of me, a pile of eyeballs reflected the light. One rolled across the floor toward me.

I stifled a scream.

18

"Scotty! Deanna! Ultraboy! This is not funny. There's enough weird stuff going on without you trying to scare me to death," I whispered urgently.

Something covered my mouth. I twisted to get free, but my fright had made me too weak. More hands grabbed me and pulled me away from the door.

"Shh. Michael, are you all right?"

"What?" I looked into Deanna's face. "Deanna?"

"Don't let those guys in the hallway hear you," she whispered.

"Aren't these eyeballs cool?" Scotty said in a low voice. "They must be models to show to patients."

I turned to get a closer look and realized the eyeballs were made out of plastic.

"Sorry we scared you. We were exploring when you came in and didn't want to make too much noise. We found another door over there that leads to a hallway," Scotty said.

"Well, what are we waiting for? Let's go," I told them.

As we shut the door behind us, I heard the door we had come in through open.

"That was close. We barely escaped," Deanna said.

"Yeah, but escaped to where?" I asked.

"That's a good question. Another good one is: Which way do we go now?" Deanna added.

Scotty pointed at a wall full of elevator doors. "Since we fell a long way in the laundry chute, why don't we try heading up?" he said.

That made sense to me. When we got off the elevator, our only option seemed to be to enter a gift shop.

We didn't say a word to each other. A gift shop sounded harmless, but then again, everything else here had sounded harmless as well. I looked in through the window to see if anyone was inside. The place looked deserted.

I headed for the door. Scotty tugged at my arm and asked, "Can't we just find the front door and get out of here?"

"That's my plan, but it looks like the only way out must be through the gift shop," I sadly said.

As we pulled the gift shop door open, I said, "Everything seems so bizarre here. What do you think is going on? Did we walk into the twilight zone or something like that? Or is this some kind of joke?"

Scotty stared at me. I knew he was thinking. He finally said, "Maybe we walked onto a horror movie set. We could be messing up the filming. That would explain why people keep chasing us."

"That doesn't make sense. We would have seen cameras and lighting equipment," I told him.

"All the riddles say that something is supposed to make you laugh, scare you to death, and somehow heal people too," Deanna said. "I just wish I knew what that something is. That book Scotty found in the library makes me wonder if the emergency room and the riddle go together. What do you guys think?"

"They might," Scotty answered. Then he asked, "Do you think that ticket we found is a clue too?"

"What did it say again?" I asked.

"I've got it right here," Deanna said as she pulled the ticket from her pocket. "'Horror f' and 'for kids.'"

"Any ideas?" I asked.

"How about 'Horror faces' or 'Horror feet'?" Scotty suggested.

Deanna added, "Horror Fruit Loops?"

We all giggled. We hadn't even looked at any of the gifts on the shelves as we passed them. We were too focused on the riddles. I absently opened the other door to the gift shop. I hoped it would take us near an exit from the hospital. Sounds from the hallway drifted through the partially open door.

"There are only a few patients in the hospital today.

I can't believe we keep losing them. In some hospitals, they would call this malpractice," a woman's voice said.

"In this hospital it should be malfright. Where do we look now?" the other voice asked.

"Stick your head in the gift shop. If they aren't in there, I guess we'll have to go back upstairs. I'm glad I'm almost done for the day."

I quickly pushed Scotty and Deanna between two aisles of trinkets. They stumbled over each other. Scotty reached out to grab something to prevent his fall. But he grabbed a shelf full of pens and pencils. They rained down on top of him in a clatter.

I only had enough time to signal them to be quiet before the door opened. We sat as still as possible. Then I realized there was one pencil left on the shelf—and it was slowly rolling toward the edge. If it fell, the noise would probably give us away.

Neither Deanna nor Scotty could move without sending the pencils all around him clattering again. I was about a foot too far away to stop the moving pencil.

I scanned the shelf for something to help me. I was surprised that everything I saw had some sort of monster face, head, or body. I didn't take the time to puzzle out why because I saw exactly what I needed. It was a monster head that extended on a scissors-like contraption. Its mouth opened and closed to pick up objects from a distance. I remembered playing with a toy like that when I was little.

I pulled the monster head from the display and stretched it toward the teetering pencil. I prayed I wouldn't miss. Scotty and Deanna held their breath as they watched me grab for the pencil that could give us away.

I managed to snag the potential threat as I heard someone leave the gift shop. The door closed loudly, and we all sighed in relief.

As Scotty stood up he looked closely at the trinkets all around us. Furrowing his eyebrows in concentration, he asked, "Have you noticed that all the stuff in this place looks like some kind of monster?"

I picked up one of the pencils. The eraser was shaped like Frankenstein's head. The next one I grabbed had Dracula at the end. Deanna moved to another shelf and called back to us. "Hey, these stuffed animals are all monsters too. This hospital is so weird. Nothing surprises me anymore."

Deanna checked out the hallway and discovered that the coast was clear. We decided we'd better get going while we could.

The corridor was quiet, and we tiptoed along. The last thing we needed was to attract anyone's attention. As we looked for a way out, I whispered, "Deanna, do you remember what Mr. Bush said in Sunday school last week?"

"Be quiet and sit up straight?" she quipped.

"No, I mean about how God is always with us," I said.

"Do you think he's with us now?" Scotty asked.

"I'm sure he is. That makes me feel like we'll get out of this okay," I answered.

Scotty said he felt better just remembering that we weren't alone. Without fear, he pushed a swinging door open. On the wall we saw two arrows. One pointed to the right and was labeled Intensive Care. The other pointed left and had the words Waiting Room.

"Which way?" Scotty asked.

Deanna answered quickly, "I would happily sit in a waiting room until your mom comes to get us."

We turned left and found the room. I saw four people sitting inside. Their backs were to us, and they were watching TV.

I quietly approached a woman and tapped her on the shoulder. "Excuse me," I said, "but we're trying to find the way out of here. Can you help us?" She didn't respond. I thought that was a little rude, but stranger things had been happening all day.

Scotty nearly made me jump out of my skin by screaming. I flinched reflexively and turned to see what had scared him.

Scotty pointed at the woman I had touched. Confused, I looked at her face. She was all bones. A skeleton? Didn't she belong in some chiropractor's office?

"I don't think that they can help us," Scotty said when he regained his composure. "In fact, I don't think they can help anyone."

Deanna scratched her head and said, "I think there should be a Surgeon General's warning posted on this hospital: It can be hazardous to your health."

Her joke would have been funnier if we weren't surrounded by folks who had hung out too long in the Waiting Room.

"I'm not into sitting with skeletons, even if they might be another clue to the riddles," Scotty said.

Another clue? I wondered. He might be right.

"I'm with you," Deanna said.

We headed back into the hall. In spite of its ominous name, we decided to explore Intensive Care. Deanna wondered how intense the care we might get there would be, but she didn't seem particularly afraid after Scotty reminded her again that God was always with us. We discovered a group of doctors and nurses when we cautiously entered. Would these be normal? Or would they turn out to be more horror flick escapees? One of the doctors waved at us and said, "Please, come in. We've been waiting for you. Which one of you is here for the transplant?"

"The what?" Scotty asked. I wished he hadn't.

"The heart transplant, of course. We've got everything ready. All we need is the patient," she said. Then she motioned with her white-coated arm toward the surgical instrument table. I noticed she had gloves on, but they weren't surgical gloves. They looked like ski gloves.

Rather than waiting for something really weird to happen, Deanna spoke up. "We're a little lost. Can you help us find our way out?"

Instead of answering, one of the orderlies moved quietly toward us. Before I realized what he was doing, he had Scotty in his grasp.

"Ultraboy, what would Ultraboy do?" Deanna pleaded as the orderly carried Scotty away.

Scotty, who had looked terrified, perked up at the mention of Ultraboy. After a moment, he glanced at me and then looked pointedly toward the wall. I looked in that direction and shook my head. I didn't understand what he wanted. He moved his head in a slight circle, and I got it. I saw two wheelchairs parked along the wall.

I snagged one by its handles and shoved it toward the orderly holding Scotty. Startled, the man let go of my brother to protect his knees.

Deanna had grabbed the other chair, and she called to Scotty to hop on. As she flew toward the door with her cargo, I ran to open it. I jumped into Scotty's lap as the chair screeched past me. Deanna held on to the handles for all she was worth and kept pushing.

We left the others in the dust and careened down the hallway. We flew past the Waiting Room entrance and kept on going. When she felt safe, Deanna slowed the chair down.

We all noticed the colored glass window at about the same time.

Curious, Deanna stood on her tiptoes and looked through the window. She wore a huge grin when she turned back to us. "You won't believe this," she said.

"Did we find the exit?" Scotty asked hopefully.

"No," she answered. "It's the hospital chapel. I'm sure we'll be safe here."

"I don't care about safe anymore. I just want to go back to the cabin in the woods," I complained.

Deanna shot me a look, and I stopped whining. I was too old to whine anyway.

Scotty interrupted us by saying, "I think I've got an answer."

"To the riddle? That's fantastic!" Deanna exclaimed.

"Not exactly, but I think I know how to solve it," he replied. "Remember when Joseph was called before the Pharaoh?"

"Yeah, but what's that got to do with a hospital gone haywire?" I asked.

"God revealed the explanation to the Pharaoh's dreams when Joseph prayed for guidance," Scotty said. "Maybe we should stop and talk to God about our situation."

Deanna and I agreed. We decided to go into the chapel to make sure we weren't interrupted.

We got settled in and had just started to ask for

God's help in solving the riddle or getting out of the hospital safely. Suddenly the door opened, and an orderly bounded toward us.

"Finally, I found you. You kids have been pretty tough to track down," he said.

Others followed him into the room.

As he grabbed Deanna, he turned to them and said, "These are the patients that everyone's been looking for. Grab them. Since they aren't playing by the rules, we'll have to keep them tied up until security gets here."

"Tied up!" Deanna exclaimed.

"He means figuratively," I said, hoping I was right. But I wasn't. A burly man ushered us out of the chapel and into an examination room. Another man in a lab coat pulled Ace bandages and adhesive tape from a utility cart.

Deanna tried to reason with them as they began to tie us up. "Doctors, I don't want to bother you, but do you realize that we don't have any insurance? Maybe you should just send us on our way."

The two simply turned their backs on us and started talking to themselves. I whispered to my cousin, "Deanna, do you have any ideas on how to get out of this one?"

She just shrugged her shoulders at me.

One of the men said to the other, "These three aren't going anywhere. I guess it's safe to leave them for security."

I was surprised that they took off. "Well, since we seem to have some time on our hands, maybe we should finish our prayer and see if we can figure out the riddle," I suggested.

Deanna started right in by thanking God for keeping us safe. Then she asked for wisdom as we continued to ponder the riddles.

I asked Scotty to recite the riddles he could remember.

He said, "Well, the first one was:

'What can make you laugh till you're out
   of breath
But still scare you to death?
What can help kids heal
While its fright makes you squeal?
What can raise change
While acting deranged?'"

"Do we have enough clues to figure this out yet?"

"Something tells me that we've been looking at this all wrong. Maybe the riddle's not talking about specific things. Maybe it's about the whole hospital," Deanna said tentatively.

"Hospitals heal," I said.

"Haunted hospitals scare," Scotty said. "But what makes us laugh?"

The door opened, and a woman carrying a cat entered. The cat jumped from her arms and skidded across the waxed floor.

"Goodness," the woman said. "Did you order the CAT scan? I'm sorry I've been running late," she apologized.

The cat danced out the door, and the woman ran after it.

"Weird," Scotty mumbled.

I chewed on my lower lip as I thought through the day's events. "I've been thinking," I finally said. "Do you remember when our youth pastor told us about that mission project?"

"Yeah, I remember," Deanna said. I could tell from her face that she had no idea what I was thinking.

"You're flipping out on us, Michael," Scotty said. "What does a summer mission project in the inner city have to do with this crazy hospital?"

"Nothing. I was just thinking about what Pastor

99

Wayne said: 'There are two kinds of people. Those who let things happen to them and those who make things happen.' I just realized that we've been letting things happen to us. I believe if we use our heads and a whole lot of caution, we can make things happen the way we want," I tried to sound like a football coach rallying his team.

"Maybe, if we work at it, we can get out of these bandages," Scotty suggested. "It's at least a start at trying to make things happen."

As she worked at her bandages, Deanna mused, "Sometimes it seems like we're in some museum of medical madness. Then it feels like a carnival fun house. By the way, the next time I get sick I want to be housebound. Don't even let me go to a doctor. Like you said earlier, Michael, hospitals make me sick."

Three security officers finally came into the room.

One had a bushy handlebar mustache. It wiggled when he said, "So, we've finally found the three of you. It's really time for us to get rid of you. I guess we'll have to untie you so you can follow us out."

Deanna's eyes had widened. She whispered to me, "Get rid of us?"

I tried to calm her with a smile as the officers untied us. When we were all free, my little brother suddenly became Ultraboy again. Scotty hurled himself onto the bed and scurried into a standing position. He taunted the three guards.

With their attention distracted, Deanna whispered to me, "This is our chance to escape. Follow Ultraboy. If we can keep the bed between us and those three, we're safe. Once we're in the hall, run for it."

The guards were so surprised by our actions that they barely responded. Or so I thought.

When we hit the hall, I discovered four orderlies were waiting for us. One of them growled down at us, "Okay, kids, I think it's time that you come with us. The end is near."

"The end for who?" Deanna yelled. She grabbed Scotty's hand and ran with all her strength. I followed at breakneck speed as our would-be captors tried to keep up.

24

Ahead of us, elevator doors had just begun to close. If we were lucky, we could slip inside and leave the others behind. Spurred on by the possibility of escape, we fairly flew.

We made it! Now I just had to decide which floor to take us to.

Scotty curled up near my feet and said, "I think I have a recurring illness."

"Like what?" I asked.

"Fear," he answered.

"So do I," added Deanna. I nodded my head in agreement.

"I want to go home," Scotty added.

"They say that a change of scenery is always healthy. I think I'd like a change, especially since this place is lousy for our health," our cousin answered.

When the elevator doors opened, I looked warily down the hallway to make sure we were alone. There wasn't much activity in this part of the hospital.

I heard faint squeaking noises up ahead and led the others toward them to explore. I peeked through a window and saw a laboratory technician working with different lab animals.

I got a good look at the cages. They were filled with dozens of white mice.

"Ooh," said Deanna, "you couldn't pay me enough to work in there. Let's keep going."

I noticed a supply room up ahead on the left and pointed it out. "There's a supply room. Maybe we can find three smaller uniforms to sneak out of here in."

"We'd blend in better that way," Deanna conceded. "With luck, no one will chase us if we're dressed like we belong here."

We slipped into the staff closet. There were lots of clean, fresh surgical scrubs neatly folded on the shelves. We pulled them on over our clothes and wrapped surgical masks around our faces. I prayed it would work this time. I noticed a stretcher on the wall. "There's a stretcher. If we act like we are going somewhere with it then no one will bother us."

Deanna gave me one of those you've-got-to-be-kidding looks, but Scotty said what was on his mind. "Michael, in this hospital there is no such thing as not being bothered. The stretcher isn't a bad idea, though. If we hurry through the halls people might think we've got an emergency and give us space."

We had a plan and were prepared to make things

happen. We opened the door carefully to make sure that no one was around. The hallway was empty. Our chance had come. I walked out pushing the stretcher, and Deanna followed me. I had Scotty walk next to it in case we needed to put someone on it as a decoy.

As we quickly strode down the hall, Scotty's stomach growled loudly, and we all laughed. "I'm really hungry," he said with an apologetic grin.

"We could always go back to the cafeteria," I suggested. But Scotty remembered the kitchen and vigorously shook his head.

A group of orderlies pushing stretchers headed our way.

"Just stay cool," I cautioned under my breath.

One of the orderlies looked at us and grumbled, "There you are. Are you three lost or something? We're supposed to be down there. Come on. Follow us." He turned away from us and mumbled to himself, "New help . . ."

We obediently followed them, retracing our steps.

The head orderly opened the door and directed us into a room. The first thing I noticed was a terrible smell. It was like rotting lunch and week-old gym clothes that had sat too long in a locker.

A large beaker sat on a Bunsen burner. Blue-green slime boiled up and over the top. I turned to one of the orderlies and asked in my best adult voice, "What is that stuff?"

"It's what we feed to the medical staff. It's made out of—well, it would be best if you could just solve the riddle and not have to find out," he said.

I knew then that he knew that we weren't doctors.

"Wait a second, guys. We'll solve the riddle. Maybe getting near that awful-smelling stuff will clear my head," I told them as I edged closer to the horrible stench. The orderlies followed me and formed a circle around me. It was just what I wanted. I looked at the table that the beaker and Bunsen burner sat on. I saw what I was looking for—a pair of tongs.

Using them I tipped the beaker over, and out poured the thick slime. I turned and yelled, "Run!" I was already moving at top speed because the ooze had begun to nip at my heels. Scotty and Deanna leaped to the door and yanked it open. I took one look over my shoulder as I followed them. The orderlies were slipping and flailing on the slime-covered floor.

We kept running down the hall. Then I noticed the colored stripes beneath my feet.

Suddenly Scotty grabbed me by the arm. "Remember that book we found in the hospital library?"

"I don't think this is the time to discuss literature," I snapped at him.

"You don't get it. I said that the three kids in the book found the way out through the Emergency Room. If I am right, this red line painted on the floor will lead us right to the Emergency Room," he added.

"How do you know that?" I asked.

"Books, dear brother. That is the power of education. Sometimes what you know can save your life," he boasted.

"Let's go," Deanna said impatiently. In a few minutes we were standing outside of the Emergency Room. We stared at each other. We all knew that we were on the edge of finding our way out. The only thing left was to solve the riddle.

I took the first step inside. People were hurrying around, but they completely ignored us. We slipped off our surgical garb and plopped down on one of the poorly padded, plastic, imitation leather couches. It felt good to rest.

Suddenly I tensed, ready to run, as a doctor walked toward us.

"Can I help you? It doesn't look like you've gotten the care you need," he said.

"Well, I am having a reaction to treatment," Deanna said.

"What kind of reaction?" the doctor asked in a serious, caring tone.

"Fear, fright, and panic," she answered.

"That's what we're here for," he said through a big smile.

"I'd rather you told us how to get out of this place instead," Scotty said.

"That shouldn't be that hard." He smiled again and then wrote some instructions on a piece of paper. He handed it to Scotty and then left us.

I was anxious to see what it said. Before the doctor was three steps away from us, I grabbed the paper from Scotty's hands and looked at it. I could not believe it. I had always heard that a doctor's handwriting was impossible to read, but this was worse than I expected. I could not read a single word the doctor had written. In my frustration, I crumpled up the paper and tossed it on the floor.

Scotty jumped up and grabbed the crumpled note. He looked at me angrily and growled, "Why did you do that?"

"Because you can't read his writing," I answered.

Scotty picked up the ball of paper and slowly smoothed it out. Then he began to study it very closely. After a few minutes he sighed. "Michael, you're right. I can barely make out a few letters, let alone read how we're supposed to get out of this place."

Deanna dropped her head into her hands in total surrender. "What are we going to do now?"

"Keep looking, I guess," was all the answer I could give.

"The only words I can read are 'look up'," Scotty added.

It hit me. I spun around and grabbed the note. "Scotty, that's it. You've solved it."

"Solved what? How?"

"Look up!" I said as I pointed upward. Directly above us was a sign that read Lobby.

Deanna and Scotty scooted off the imitation leather couch. We just about ran through the doorway. I could see the sunlight coming through glass doors.

From behind us boomed a voice, "I hope your hospital stay has been pleasant."

"What?" the three of us said in unison.

A large nurse dressed in a starched white uniform was standing behind us. She had a gigantic smile. How could this woman think that crazy doctors chasing us and trying to remove our organs was pleasant?

Deanna smiled at her and said, "Yeah, great fun. I can't wait for my next hospital visit."

The nurse kept smiling and talking. "You know, we have so many kids say that. Some even want us to make house calls. Can you believe it? Well, anyway, will you kids be sure that you tell others about us? We would love to have more patients."

"Yeah, we can do that. We'll tell everyone we know about this place and how important it is to take care of their health. In fact, I know I'm going to do a lot more preventive maintenance like I've been taught," Deanna said.

The nurse kept on smiling. She seemed to have nothing else to say. We smiled back and left. I was taking the longest strides I could in order to get out of the hospital quickly. The door was in sight when I heard Scotty's soft call for help.

I turned around, and my brother was in the grip of a doctor.

27

Deanna and I froze. The front door was so close, but I wasn't going through it without my brother at my side. The doctor looked familiar. It was the same one we met when we first came in.

"I wanted to see how the elbow looks," he told us. He looked under the bandage. "It looks like you could use a fresh bandage. This will only take a minute," he said.

"That's all right. Our mother is waiting outside. I'm sure she has some bandages at home," I argued, but I could see it was going to get us nowhere.

I stood and watched as the doctor repatched Scotty's elbow. Deanna asked in her usual bluntness, "Doctor, I thought they called you a vet when you were paged?"

"Typical joke around this place. The people here have their hearts in the right place. Well, this looks like it should do the job," he told us as he finished with the new bandage. "See you again sometime.

Oh, by the way, did you solve the riddle? You know I really can't let you leave unless you have."

"Oh, yeah, the riddle. This place is a lot of fun, and it makes kids better while it scares us to death. It's been a real scream. Kind of like a funhouse for maniacs," Deanna said.

It hit me! *Thank you, Lord, for the answer.*

Scotty and Deanna looked at me strangely. The doctor smiled from ear to ear and asked, "What is the answer, then?"

"This place is like a big funhouse. We were supposed to laugh at all the crazy stuff. You must be doing it to raise money—change—to help kids get better," I told the doctor.

"That's it. We'll be tearing down this old hospital in a few weeks when the new Children's Health Center is done. I hope you enjoyed yourselves. It's been a real scream for all of us at the hospital. And remember our motto: Horror funhouse for kids. It's on your tickets." He then turned and left us. Inside my head I was thanking the Lord over and over again. He had given me the answer, just like he always does when we listen.

"I'm not wasting another second. I want out of this place no matter what its real purpose is," I said as I jogged toward the front door. I waited. I half expected some unusual beast to grab me at any time. Nothing happened. As I pushed on the door, the doctor called out, "Tell your mom the bandage was on the house, but we would appreciate a donation toward the new facility."

"No prob, Doc," I said, pushing through the front door and out into the parking lot.

Scotty and Deanna were right there behind me. When we walked out into the center of the parking lot, Mom's car pulled in. I waved to her, and she pulled up next to us. Scotty and Deanna climbed in the backseat, and I jumped up front.

"Good timing," Mom said. "I just need to run in and pay your bill before we take off."

"You don't need to. The doctor said the bandage was on the house but they'd appreciate a donation for their new Children's Health Center," I told her.

"That was nice of them. I'll write them a check and mail it in," she said with a grin as she pulled away from the building.

We were about halfway across the lot when Mom stopped the car. "I forgot to check Scotty's elbow. Bring it up so I can see what the doctor did. Did he give you any stitches?" she asked.

"No, he just cleaned it and patched it," Scotty told her.

"Mom, could you get us out of here," I pleaded.

"I know what you mean. I'm sorry I took so long, but that little business deal will feed us for several months. Speaking of that, I'll bet you three are starved. I heard about a nice little restaurant in town. Why don't we go there?" she continued talking as she settled herself back behind the wheel. "So, what did you do while I was gone? I'll bet you had a boring wait."

"You wouldn't believe it if we told you, Mom," I said.

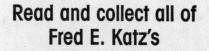

A Haunted Mine Is a Terrible Thing to Waste

Book #12
by Fred E. Katz

**When a group from their church
sets out to rebuild an old mining town as a
Christian summer camp, Boone and Cali find
themselves on a scary adventure that
leads them into a deserted mine.**

**Are the noises inside coming
from the unknown beast that is said to
roam the surrounding woods?**

"Is this Camp Fearless?" I asked, staring at the remains of a dozen or so old buildings.

"Yep, Boone, it sure is. Looks like it needs a little work, doesn't it?" said Mr. Ramos, my neighbor.

"I'd say it needs a *lot* of work," I said.

"I guess if you didn't have any tender loving care for fifty years, you'd look a little run down too," Mr. Ramos said as he stopped in front of one of the old buildings.

"Mr. Ramos, why hasn't anyone lived in this town for so long?" I asked.

"No one's lived here since the old mine ran dry.

"Remember Mr. Markham from church?" Mr. Ramos said. "He's owned the town of Fearless for years, but he's never done any repair work here. If he had, he might have sold it instead of donating it to the church."

"And if he hadn't donated the land, we'd still be looking for a place to hold our church camp," I added.

"Right. Let's get out and have a look. I guess we're the first to get here."

"Doesn't look much like the church camp I went to last summer," I remarked as I climbed out of the pickup.

"I guess not, but with some hard work we can make this place great," Mr. Ramos encouraged.

I had a hard time believing Camp Fearless would ever look good. "How many people are coming to help?" I asked.

"We've got seven men and women from the church. And Cali Bittner is coming with her parents," he answered.

I counted . . . ten total. With only eight adults and two middle schoolers, I found it hard to believe that we'd even scratch the surface this weekend.

I had to admit that having Cali along would make the job a lot more fun. When our Sunday school class collected food for the needy last Thanksgiving, we'd been partners. We collected more than any other team. And we had a great time working together.

I stepped onto the front porch of one of the cabins to look inside. My weight made the floorboard creak. For a moment I thought it sounded like a wild animal's cry. A chill worked its way up my spine.

I decided to blame my shiver on the cold. But as I walked to the truck, something made me look back over my shoulder. For just a second, I was certain someone was watching me from the woods.

I tried to shake off the feeling as I put on my jacket.

"Come over and look at this," Mr. Ramos called to me across the camp.

I jogged over to where he stood.

"Know what this is?" he asked.

I studied the round stone wheel and shook my head. "I don't think so," I admitted. "Can you tell me?"

"It's an old grindstone," he said. "It was probably used to sharpen tools like shovels and hoes."

"And axes," said a low voice behind me.

I jumped and turned toward the voice. Even Mr. Ramos seemed to snap to attention.

An older man with white hair stood behind us. I wondered how he had gotten there without our hearing him. His body looked thin and hunched over, and he hadn't shaved for several days. When he smiled, I saw that he was missing a front tooth.

"Ezra Pike's the name," the man said as he offered his hand to Mr. Ramos. "I sorta keep my eye on the old place. Kinda like a caretaker, I reckon."

"Nice to meet you. We didn't expect to find anyone up here. I'm Luis Ramos, and this is my young neighbor and friend Boone Colby."

"Ya'll here as part of the church-goin' folks that are plannin' on fixin' this place up?" he asked.

"Yes, sir," Mr. Ramos said with a smile. "And it looks like we've got our work cut out for us."

"Joshua Markham told me that you plan on openin' up camp by July," the old man remarked.

"God willing, that is our target date," Mr. Ramos agreed.

Ezra Pike shook his white hair and rubbed a rough hand over the stubble on his chin. "I 'spect ya won't be seein' that dream come true. Not unless ya got a right big group of people comin' ta help. These old cabins need lotsa work."

"This weekend we're just going to focus on one building—to be used as a dining hall. Our campers will sleep in tents until we have the time and money to rebuild the cabins," Mr. Ramos told the older man.

"Don't know as I'd wanna sleep in a tent up here," the older man said. His gaze took in the town, then he looked right at me. "Not with what I know about this ol' ghost town."

"Ghost town?" I blurted out.

"Don't get too excited, Boone, a ghost town is just one that nobody lives in any longer," Mr. Ramos said quickly. "This used to be a bustling mining town. But when the mine dried up, the people moved out. That doesn't mean there are ghosts here."

The caretaker gave a little laugh. "I didn't say there were any ghosts." He hesitated a moment as if thinking, then added, "Other things, maybe. But no ghosts that I've seen as of yet." The old man placed his hand on my shoulder and asked, "How old are ya then, young man?"

"Twelve, sir," I answered, glad the subject had

moved off ghosts, or whatever the caretaker thought he'd seen in Fearless.

Without warning, the old man turned and began to walk away. "I'll leave ya to yer work. If ya'll need anything, give a holler. I live in the cabin yonder, across the stream," he said as he left us.

Mr. Ramos and I looked at each other, confused by this man's sudden actions.

Ezra Pike had walked about a hundred yards away when he suddenly turned and headed back again. "Nearly forgot to tell ya what I come ta tell ya. The water in the well is sweet and good ta drink, but ya gotta git it up by pumpin' that handle," he said as he indicated the pump. Oh, and one other thing." He stopped for a moment and took in a deep breath. "The land belonging to Fearless runs to the top of that ridge." He pointed as he spoke.

I turned to look at the beautiful mountain ridge that bordered Camp Fearless.

Mr. Pike continued, "You church folk can hike any-where this side of that there ridge. It belongs to you now. Just don't cross over it. The land beyond is the Atlas Ski Resort's. And they don't cotton ta folks traipsin' on their property."

"I'll tell the others," Mr. Ramos promised.

"Good. Well I'll be gettin' along," the caretaker said. He pulled a red handkerchief from his back pocket and wiped his brow as he strolled away.

After Mr. Pike crossed the stream, Mr. Ramos looked for the best building to convert to a dining hall, and I watched out for the mysterious "other things" Ezra Pike had warned us about.

I kept one eye on the woods around us and the other on the windows of the various buildings. There was something about Fearless I didn't like. Something felt wrong in this old mining town. I knew there was a mystery here to solve. I couldn't wait for Cali to arrive to help me.